MW01145455

A Different Kind of Friend

Lake Road Library
AR Level: 4.9

AR Test Points: 0.5

AR Test Number:
25010

LAKE ROAD SCHOOL

A Different Kind of Friend

By

Angie Stafford

Illustrated by

Jane Lenoir

Ozark Publishing, Inc.
P.O. Box 228
Prairie Grove, AR 72753

Be# 1670705

Library of Congress cataloging-in-publication data

Stafford, Angie, 1963-
    A different kind of friend / by Angie Stafford ;
illustrated by Jane Lenoir.
        p.   cm.
    Summary: Angie and her horse Dunnie Bar are
special friends and win many competitions
together, until Angie makes a big mistake and sells
Dunnie Bar to someone else.
    ISBN 1-56763-295-5 (cloth : alk. paper). — ISBN
1-56763-296-3 (paper : alk. paper)
    [1. Horses—Fiction.   2. Friendship—Fiction.]
I. Lenoir, Jane, 1950-   ill.   II. Title.
PZ7.S777Di   1997
[Fic]—dc20   96-34169
                                            CIP
                                            AC

Copyright © 1997 by Angie Stafford
All rights reserved

Printed in the United States of America

iv

Inspiration

This is a true story about the love between a horse and his owner. The horse is truly one of a kind and will always be a winner.

Dedicated to

all my family and friends

Foreword

A young girl and a horse become very close friends. The two find each other and then become separated. They eventually get together once again and rekindle their friendship. They both love each other and the sport of barrel racing.

A Different Kind of Friend

Once in a lifetime we find a special friend. One young girl named Angie found that friend in a magnificent horse called Dunnie Bar.

Angie wanted a great horse more than anything in the world. Every day she found herself daydreaming about this special horse. She told her friends and family, "One day I will find the fastest, smartest horse in the country, and he will be mine."

The day finally arrived when Angie's dream came true. She was visiting some friends when she laid eyes upon the most beautiful horse she had ever seen. The horse was running wildly in an enormous field. Angie immediately noticed his strong muscular build and his ability

to glide across the field as if he were
an airplane in flight. His body was
a yellowish-tan color that glowed in
the morning sun. The horse's long
mane was light brown with a soft
touch of red. He was definitely a
gorgeous animal.

Angie quickly contacted the owner and asked if the horse could be purchased. The owner said, "Yes, I will sell my horse to you, but you must promise to give him a good home." Angie agreed to give the horse a good home if the owner would sell him for a fair price. After a short discussion, the owner consented to the arrangement, and the horse became Angie's.

Angie named the horse Dunnie Bar because of his unusual color. The horse turned out to be extremely athletic and spirited. He was a natural competitor. Angie took very good care of her horse. She brushed his hair each day until it would shine. She gave him fresh food and water twice a day. She also exercised him daily on a strict schedule.

Dunnie Bar and Angie began to develop a great friendship and trust. The two became very dependent upon each other. If Angie had a problem, she would talk to Dunnie Bar. Even though he was only a horse, he made her feel safe and happy. Angie never knew she could develop such a relationship with an animal.

One day Angie heard about a barrel competition in San Antonio, Texas. A barrel competition consists of a person riding a horse as fast as possible around three barrels set in a cloverleaf pattern in the center of a show ring. Winning the competition

8

LAKE ROAD SCHOOL

would pay a great deal of money.
Angie had tremendous faith in
Dunnie Bar's athletic ability, so she
decided to enter the contest.

The two were very dedicated,
therefore they practiced the barrels
every day. At first Angie took
Dunnie Bar around the barrels very
slowly, so he could learn the pattern.

Eventually Dunnie Bar was able to go faster and faster, until one day Angie knew he was ready to compete. The two had become quite a team, each depending on the other to do their very best.

The night before the competition, Angie was very nervous, because she had never been to anything like this before. There were so many experienced riders and outstanding horses. Angie began to feel a little inferior, but then she remembered they were a team. They had formed a special friendship. She knew they could win.

The day of the competition turned out to be very cold and rainy. When Angie began to prepare Dunnie Bar for the race, they were both shivering from the extreme cold and a slight nervousness. They awaited their turn at the starting gate with little patience. The pressure began to build. The announcer called their names. It was their turn to perform. They were off!

Dunnie Bar ran faster than ever before. Angie rode on his back with great ease and ability. They turned each barrel with a tight squeeze, and then they were off to cross the finish line. The team felt a tremendous freedom and happiness as they crossed the finish line. The crowd

cheered, because the two had run the fastest time of the day. Angie and Dunnie Bar were overjoyed. Their persistence and dedication had paid off. They became champions for the day.

Angie and Dunnie Bar competed in many races after San Antonio. They became very close friends, but one sad day an unbelievable thing happened. Another girl offered Angie a great deal of money for Dunnie Bar. Angie loved her friend, but she decided to sell him to the girl. At the time Angie didn't understand what a mistake she was about to make. She did not realize friendship and love should be more important than money or prestige. She bought many horses after that, but not one could compare to Dunnie Bar. He was the one special horse in her life.

Dunnie Bar was very sad. He went to another girl who did not care for him nearly as well as Angie.

She fed him, but she did not brush
his hair or exercise him every day.
He became very depressed. The
new owner would even whip him if
he were to misbehave. Dunnie Bar
would dream at night of his old
home with Angie and his once great
happiness. He wanted only to see
his friend again.

One cold day in November Angie and Dunnie Bar were able to unite once again. The new owner called Angie and said, "I want to sell Dunnie Bar. He is no longer able to win in competition." Angie agreed to buy Dunnie Bar back and keep him for herself, because she knew he was a true friend.

Angie and the owner met in Cleburne, Texas, so Angie could get the horse. Dunnie Bar went to live with Angie, where he became her special horse just as before. The two quickly became a team once again. They went to many barrel competitions and won first place. The bond between them had remained even though it had been five years. They were full of joy to be reunited!

Angie and Dunnie Bar stayed together for many years. They had many exciting times together as companions. They never forgot each other or their special friend-ship. They both learned it was bet-ter to have had one special friend in your life than to have never felt that

love at all. They will always look back on their times together and feel a great sense of happiness and joy. Sometimes we find true friends in the most unusual places.

LAKE ROAD SCHOOL